# Howard B. Wigglebottom
## and Manners Matters

**Howard Binkow    Reverend Ana**

**Illustrations by Taillefer Long**

Howard B. Wigglebottom woke up very worried.

The Pup Scouts' Good Manners Competition is in five days, and his team is not ready—at all!

3

Oinky keeps forgetting to say "excuse me" when he burps or passes gas.

4

That is not nice!

Joey does not say "excuse me" when he bumps into people.

That is not nice!

Kiki needs to learn words that make people feel good.

8

She is not nice.

The Snorton twins have trouble waiting their turn and cut in line.

That is not nice, either.

Buzz coughs without covering his mouth and does not wash his hands after going to the bathroom.

That is not nice, and dangerous, too!

Poochie—so uncool and not nice—

14

still says bad words when he is angry.

And Ali does not say "excuse me" when she interrupts grownups.

HOME 79 TIME
VISITORS 80 0:01

That is not nice!

"How can the team get ready in time for the competition?" thought Howard.
"We are so behind."

"How about a really good coach?" said the little voice in his head. "Every
team needs a coach!"

Howard listened!

After asking several grownups for help, Howard found the best manners
coach ever: Ms. Owlee.

Howard was very excited! The team was going to learn good manners for good—besides doing well in the competition!

Ms. Owlee got to work right away. She watched each kid's manners at home, school, the park, and stores. Everyone on the team needed better manners.

"To have good manners is to do what makes people feel good and comfortable," she said. Then, she told the team a little secret: "To have the best manners ever, we must repeat the magical little words 'I care.' Repeat them many, many times: 'I care, I care, I care.'"

AHH...CHOO!!

I care.
Sorry for not
covering my face.

"Now," Ms. Owlee said, "let us go out there and practice 'I care.'"

Four days later, Ms. Owlee's magical little words had worked wonders.

The team's manners had gone from bad to great!

A funny thing happened, too.

The kids felt really happy about themselves as they practiced making others feel good and comfortable.

29

And, yes, they did really well at the competition!

# Howard B. Wigglebottom and Manners Matters
## Suggestions for Lessons and Reflections

To have good manners means to be nice. That means doing only things that make people feel good and comfortable:

- Say "please" when we ask for something.

- Say "thank you" when we get what we asked for or when someone does something nice for us.

- Say "excuse me, I'm sorry" when we burp, pass gas, sneeze, or cough.

- Say "excuse me, I'm sorry" if we bump into someone or break things by mistake.

- Say "excuse me, please" if we have to interrupt adults.

- Cover our faces when we burp, sneeze, or cough.

- Wash our hands every time we go to the bathroom.

- Knock on closed doors and wait for an answer before opening them.

- Wait for our turn to speak or play a game, and when in line.

- Hold open the door when someone is right behind us.

- Only use good words when talking to or about people.

Seem like a lot to remember? Practice every day and, soon, it will be very easy! Ask your teacher and someone in your household to help you!

Why should we wash our hands after going to the bathroom and cover our faces when we cough or sneeze? Because bathrooms, sneezes, and coughs have germs, cooties that can make us sick.

Why should we use only good words when talking to or about people? Because bad words hurt. Good words to use when talking to or about people are "you are pretty," "she is nice," "he is a friend," "you are smart," "we are good," and "I like you." Can you think of more good words to say to people?

What did the manners coach teach the team? To care means to say nice things about and do nice things to or for people, because everyone has feelings.

What nice things can you do to or for people around you today to show you care?

For help with teaching your children good manners, please visit wedolisten.org and click on the Manners Matters interactive lesson.

Howard Binkow  Reverend Ana
Illustration by Taillefer Long
Book design by Jane Darroch Riley

Thunderbolt Publishing
We Do Listen Foundation
www.wedolisten.org

Learn more about Howard's other adventures.

## BOOKS

*Howard B. Wigglebottom Learns to Listen*
*Howard B. Wigglebottom Listens to His Heart*
*Howard B. Wigglebottom Learns About Bullies*
*Howard B. Wigglebottom Learns About Mud and Rainbows, When Parents Fight*
*Howard B. Wigglebottom Learns It's OK to Back Away*
*Howard B. Wigglebottom and the Monkey on His Back: A Tale About Telling the Truth*
*Howard B. Wigglebottom and the Power of Giving: A Christmas Story*
*Howard B. Wigglebottom Learns Too Much of a Good Thing Is Bad*
*Howard B. Wigglebottom Blends in Like Chameleons: A Fable About Belonging*
*Howard B. Wigglebottom Learns About Sportsmanship: Winning Isn't Everything*
*Howard B. Wigglebottom Learns About Courage*
*Howard B. Wigglebottom On Yes or No: A Fable About Trust*

## WEB SITE

Visit www.wedolisten.org:
• Enjoy free animated books, games, and songs.
• Print lessons and posters from the books, and contact us.

## THANKS

Our special gratitude goes to the following people:
Cindy Hebert;  Joanne, Sophia and Eric De Graaf; and Rosemary Underwood–their comments made the book much better!

Appreciation and gratitude are also given to those volunteers who gave us feedback and the schools that participated in the review process:
Alamance Christian School, Graham, North Carolina; Christ Church School, Ft. Lauderdale, Florida;
Greater Summit County Early Learning Center, Akron, Ohio; Lamarque Elementary, Northport, Florida; Luther Vaughn Elementary,
Gaffney, South Carolina; S.C.O.P.E. Academy Preschool, Akron, Ohio; Suncoast Schools for Innovative Studies, Sarasota, Florida;
and Woburn Junior Public School, Toronto, Canada.

First printing June 2013
Printed in Malaysia by Tien Wah Press (Pte) Limited.

ISBN  978-0-9826165-9-8

LCCN 210393907